Topic: Interpersonal Skills   **Subtopic:** Empathy

Notes to Parents and Teachers:

As a child becomes more familiar reading books, it is important for them to rely on and use reading strategies more independently to help figure out words they do not know.

REMEMBER: PRAISE IS A GREAT MOTIVATOR!

Here are some praise points for beginning readers:

• I saw you get your mouth ready to say the first letter of that word.

• I like the way you used the picture to help you figure out that word.

• I noticed that you saw some sight words you knew how to read!

Book Ends for the Reader!

Here are some reminders before reading the text:

• Point to each word you read to make it match what you say.

• Use the picture for help.

• Look at and say the first letter sound of the word.

• Look for sight words that you know how to read in the story.

• Think about the story to see what word might make sense.

Words to Know Before You Read

card

cheer

dance

friendship

outside

phone

rocks

unicorn

How to Be
Friends with This Unicorn

By Erin Savory
Illustrated by Ana Zurita

I met Luma in the forest.

4

Luma is a unicorn.

They like to spend time in the forest.

They are a great dancer. We have a special friendship dance.

I want to visit Luma.
But they are not
feeling well.

8

How can I be friends with this unicorn?

Luma needs to rest.
They cannot play outside.
I collect pretty rocks for Luma.

10

I write a letter to my friend.
I bring it to cheer Luma up.

I wonder how
Luma is feeling.

My mom helps me call
them on the phone.

We have fun talking.

We even do our dance.

We have to change it a little, but it's OK.

Luma feels good today.
They made me a card.

18

They thanked me for cheering them up.

How can you be friends with
this unicorn?

Show them you care.

Luma cares about their friends too!

Book Ends for the Reader

"I know..."
Why does Luma need to stay home?

"I think..."
How do you feel when you are sick and cannot play?

What happened in this book?
Look at each picture and talk about what happened in the story.

About the Author

Erin Savory is a writer who lives in Florida. She loves to paint with her two-year-old son. She loves spending time in nature. Reading is her favorite activity.

About the Illustrator

Ana Zurita was born by the sea in Valencia, Spain, where she completed her studies in Fine Arts and currently lives with her wonderful family. She is a big fan of the beach in winter, the color yellow, the smell of old books, and heavy blankets. But what has made her the happiest from a very early age is drawing. That's why her greatest dream is to make others happy with her illustrations.

Library of Congress PCN Data

How to Be Friends with This Unicorn / Erin Savory
(How to Be Friends)
ISBN 978-1-73164-344-5 (hard cover)(alk. paper)
ISBN 978-1-73164-308-7 (soft cover)
ISBN 978-1-73164-376-6 (e-Book)
ISBN 978-1-73164-408-4 (ePub)
Library of Congress Control Number: 2020945207

Rourke Educational Media
Printed in the United States of America
01-3502011937

© 2021 Rourke Educational Media

www.rourkeeducationalmedia.com

Edited by: Tracie Santos
Layout by: Morgan Burnside
Cover and interior illustrations by: Ana Zurita